My Friends
Make Me Happy

By WANDA HAYES   **Pictures by FRANCES HOOK**

ISBN: 0-87239-351-8

STANDARD PUBLISHING

Cincinnati, Ohio   3621

The Doctor

"Right this way," says the nurse in a pretty
    white dress.
    (Even her stockings are white.)
"Stand on the scale, and I'll see what you weigh.
    Then I'll measure to find your true height.

"You're forty-four pounds heavy today,
    Thirty-nine and one-half inches tall.
Sit right up here till the doctor comes in."
    (That's when I look at the wall.)

"Hello, young man. Let me look at your throat."
    "Ahh!" I say, doing my part.
With his 'scope on my chest, he plugs in his ears
    And hears each beat of my heart.

He looks in my eyes, my ears, and my nose,
    And flashes a tiny white light.
"Young man, that's all on this visit for you.
    I'm glad to say you're all right."

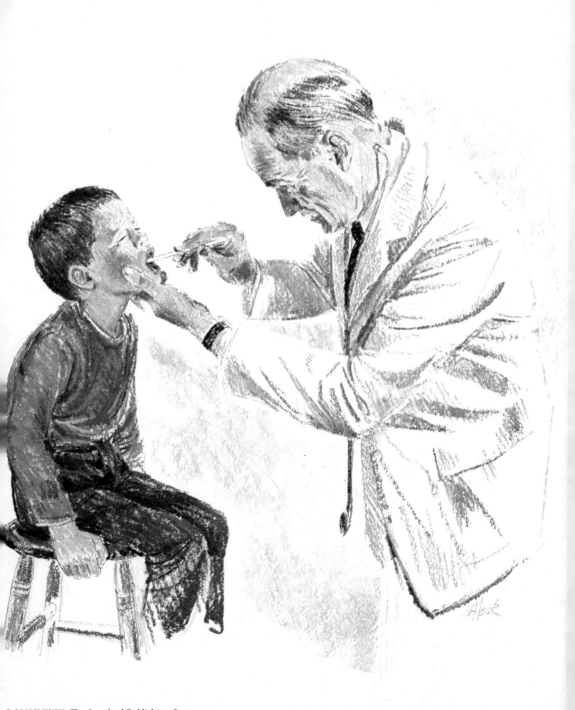

The Shoe Lady

"Good morning, Shoe Lady.
   Yes, I'm okay.
Guess what kind of shoes
   I'm buying today?"

"Are they soft, red shoes to help you run
   Outside and inside for all kinds of fun?"
"No, Miss Shoe Lady,
   Not soft shoes today."

"Maybe you're going to buy shiny, brown shoes.
   I think shoes for good are the kind you'll
      choose."
"No, they aren't shoes for good that I want in
      your store.
   They're for someplace I never have gone to
      before."

"I know," she said with a glow in her eyes.
   "You're going to school—you're just the size."
She hurried away and came back with a pair
Of sturdy leather shoes like all school kids wear.

Friends at the Zoo

If I saw my friends at the zoo every day,
  I would teach them how to play games.
They could do tricks especially for me,
  And I'd call them by their first names.

Perhaps I could slide down Jill Giraffe's neck
  And swing with the apes in a tree.
Theophilus Tiger could leap over barrels
  And growl because he is free.

"My name is Noah," I'd tell them,
  "And we're going to take a big trip.
Bring a partner and follow me,
  You're going to ride on my ship."

But I visit the zoo only once in a while,
  And some of my friends are too wild
To be allowed out of their cages
  Just to play with a child.

Friends at Play

Jump-a-rope, skip-a-rope.
  Chant a funny rhyme.
If you miss, you lose your turn.
  Jump another time.

Hop-a-scotch, hop-a-scotch.
  Roll a stone and hop.
Step on every number.
  Turn around and stop.

Hide 'n seek. Don't you peek.
  Count to ninety-three.
Find them 'round the haystack,
  Before they shout "home free."

A meadow in the country.
  A sidewalk in the town.
Happy children playing
  Until the sun goes down.

My Sister

Sister and I are good friends. On Saturday morning we clean our room. Later we play together.

"It's raining! Play in your room," Mother told us.

"What can we do?" Sister asked. "Want to look at our new library books?"

"No," I shook my head. "I don't want to read."

"Listen to records?" "No."

"Draw?" "And paint," I quickly add.

All afternoon we splashed on color after color. Then Sister put her hand on top of the easel so that her fingers hung over on my side. Splash! I got her with my brush.

"Okay for you," said Sister; and she splashed some over the top and down on me and my picture. Then we chased each other all over the room. Soon there was paint all over Sister, me, the floor, walls, and Mother standing in the doorway.

My sister and I are good friends. We work together, play together, and sometimes we get punished together.

My Mother

My mother loves me.

Every day she gives me a big hug and kiss and says, "I love you." That is just one way I know.

My mother loves me.

She cooks and irons and does all the things that mothers usually do.

My mother loves me.

She lets me go shopping with her. I choose a dress pattern and material that I like. She makes me a dress.

My mother loves me.

She makes sure that I eat good food and get enough rest and exercise. She takes me to see the doctor to make sure that I'm all right.

My mother loves me.

I would know it if she never said it.

Being Kind at School

My mother says, "If you want to make people happy, be kind to them."

"Be kind" means to treat them in a special way. That's a good way to tell another child "I like you. I want to be your friend." Some children don't know how to be kind. They can learn from you and me.

These are some ways I thought of to be kind to children at school.

Walk to the drinking fountain without pushing or shoving to get in front of someone else.

Watch out for smaller children on the playground.

Let someone else be first when playing a game.

Share crayons, pencils, paper, books, and paste.

Be quiet during quiet times.

I should also be kind to my teacher, who is always kind to me.

My Teacher at School

My teacher is my special friend at school. My teacher is very smart. She knows what bus I ride home and where to catch it . . . how much milk money I have . . . what time it is . . . how many minutes till recess . . . where the principal's office is . . . how to read cursive writing . . . how to read very well (she reads lots of stories to us) . . . why some boys and girls are late (dawdlers) . . . what boy is hiding in the coat room . . . who is giggling on the other side of the room . . . what makes my pictures pretty . . . how to play the piano and sing . . . how to make bad boys and girls behave . . . what my favorite poem is . . . how to paste without smearing . . . how to stand when we say the pledge of allegiance . . . what we can make for our parents to make them glad . . . what library books we would enjoy reading . . . what we can do when we finish our work . . . and how to make us smile.

My teacher knows a lot more than I do. She knows more than anyone else in our room. I guess that's why she's the teacher.

Worshiping at Church

Tell God you love Him.
Sing Him a song.

I love You, God.
I love You.

Thank God for blessings.
Pray to Him.

Thank You, God.
Thank You.

Give something to God.
Give Him an offering.

This is for You, God.
This is for You.

Money buys a Bible, a songbook, a chair.
We give our offering, and then we all share
The things that it buys for Your church.

This is Your church, God.
This is for You.

My Teacher at Church

It is a very special day each week when I put on my good clothes and go to our church. That's where I hear the best storyteller in the whole world, Miss Alice.

Miss Alice always smiles. "Good morning," she says when I come into the room. She talks with each one of us before it's time to get quiet. She teaches us lots of things—songs, learning games, and things to make. But my favorite time of all is when she tells a story. Her stories are special. They all come from one big book, and they're all true. "This is a very special book," Miss Alice tells us. "This is the Bible, and it is a gift from God."

Every week she tells a different story. When she tells one, everyone listens. I like to close my eyes and try to imagine what the people she talks about look like.

Sometimes when Miss Alice finishes and everyone is quiet, I think I'm still visiting the land she told us about in the story.

My special friend, Miss Alice, helps make my day at church a happy and special day.

My Friend Jesus

Dear Jesus, You are my closest friend. You are different from everyone else I know.

When I read Your words from the Bible, I feel as though You are here talking to me.

I trust You, Jesus, because You always told the truth. You did many wonderful things. You made sick people well. You made dead people alive. I'm thankful that You came to die so that my sins can be forgiven. I'm especially glad that God made You alive again.

I know that You, Jesus, will listen to me when no one else will. Although I cannot hear Your voice, I know that You understand me when no one else seems to. When I'm sorry for disobeying You, You forgive me. You still love me.

I have a special feeling wherever I am because I feel that you are nearby. You care about what I do and say, even when I'm away from church and from home.

I know about You because I read about You in the Bible. Dear Jesus, I never want to disappoint You because You never disappoint me—and I know that You never will.

My Neighbor

One day Brother and I went to see Miss Lilly.
"I'm setting out flowers," she said. "How
would you both like to plant a red one?"
When we finished, she said, "Come in and
wash your hands. I think I have just the right
food to help a working boy and girl to grow."